FOOLKILLERS

AN EVE OF LIGHT SHORT STORY

HARAMBEE K. GREY-SUN

HYPERVERSE BOOKS, LLC

ALSO BY HARAMBEE K. GREY-SUN

Standalone Stories

Beholder

Love Among the Ultramoderns

The *EVE OF LIGHT* Series

The Novels

BloodLight: The Apocalypse of Robert Goldner (*Prequel*)

Broken Angels (*Book I*)

Divinities, Entangled (*Book II*)

The Short Stories

FoolKillers

The Lark

Heaven's Gun

Knotty & Ice

Rogue Beauty

Deviant-Hunter's Sabbath

BY HARAMBEE GREY-SUN

Poetry

Spring's Fall (Autumn Numbers * Book I)

Wine Songs, Vinegar Verses

Cover design by Laura Gordon.

ISBN-13: 978-1-64044-905-3

Published by **HyperVerse Books, LLC**

www.hyperversebooks.com

writing between and beyond the lines

FOOLKILLERS

Avery Brocus should've used his real photo. He shouldn't have used his real name.

His fingers tapped the screen of his smartphone, lying flat on the table. A nervous tic. He wanted badly to text a buddy, asking him to run down and meet him at the wine bar. He needed a friend sitting at a nearby table, observing silently and ready to jump in if, instead of a young woman, some big bruiser showed up to blackmail or rob him.

Many thoughts breezed through as he waited for his kinda-sorta blind date to arrive, but the thought that he was being set up was like a tornado in his mind. He was almost dizzy with dread.

Avery wasn't entirely clear on what pushed him to set up a profile on the Freakfinder site. Curiosity was certainly a factor. He'd been hearing about hook-up websites for years, and Freakfinder was the one that promised the most success (or your money back). Loneliness wasn't the issue. Sober or tipsy he always swore he was—and *felt* he was—happy living alone with two cats. While setting up his profile, he'd muttered something to himself about satisfying an urge, scratching an itch that was more irritating than mere curiosity.

In seventeen years of legal adulthood, he'd never had a relationship last more than six weeks. He never found his dates wholly appealing. Oftentimes the feeling was more than mutual. Sometimes he'd try to stick with a woman that shared similar interests since, the older he got, the more uncomfortable he felt going to dinner or attending a show alone. But no matter how many shared interests, after a while the woman's presence began to grate, the phone calls and texting became a nuisance, and the meet-ups a chore akin to cleaning the bathroom after a week of neglect. He went on hiatus to concentrate on his job and to figure himself out. After about a year, he had an epiphany: he wasn't attracted to women his own age. He just plain didn't like what his generation was into, what they talked about, their hang-outs or their hang-ups. He wasn't a man of his time. He wanted difference. He wanted exoticism. He had a *fetish.*

In second grade, he once had a substitute teacher named Ms. Lovelace. Blonde, blue eyes, long legs, and curvy in all the right places. He couldn't believe her name or her looks, but he believed that's when it all started, his yearning for older women—women at least fifteen years older than he. Beyond taboo, he'd more than an inkling that this was perverse. He tried to suppress it, but the inclination stayed with him through high school and college. Older women turned his head and held his attention several seconds longer than the women in his peer group.

In his early thirties, when he was finally ready to give up and admit it to himself (if no one else), he started to indulge a little. He began scouring the web and watching MILF porn at midnight before crawling into bed at two a.m. A month later he graduated to hot-and-frisky granny porn. After two years of watching this stuff almost every night, he couldn't take it anymore. He wanted the real thing.

One night, after two glasses of Pinot, rather than clicking on his favorite porn site, he searched for hook-up sites catering to those who wanted to explore beyond their own age range. His profile was nothing special, though he made sure the first sentence highlighted the fact he was drug-, disease-, and drama-free. His username was PurplePet8er— a twist on a second-grader's joke. He posted pictures of a physique sculpted by five hundred push-ups a day. The pics were all nude, but they didn't venture below the waist or higher than the chin.

Over the course of two months, he clicked "like" on several dozen profiles, received one half-hearted response for every eight emails he sent, and added about a dozen reasonably attractive divorcees and attached-but-looking cougars to his hotlist. Then, he saw her profile. She wasn't in his preferred range, but those eyes . . . that face . . . Both seemed to glow. She was twenty-two, thirteen years his junior, and judging by her detailed profile, she seemed far more sexually experienced than he was sure he ever wanted to be. But he sent her a "wink." The next night he added her to his hotlist. The following night, an email: *You're beautiful. I'd wish I'd met you in another life.* The following night, he received an email: *What's wrong with this one?*

A conversation started. Sentences were volleyed before paragraphs were carefully composed and exchanged. One night, after four glasses of Pinot, when he was about to hit "send" on a 3,000 word email, he deleted it and sent two words instead. *Wanna meet?*

Yes, of course. But send me a face pic first, and tell me your name :)

He'd panicked. His body reflected the efforts of a gym rat, while his face looked like it had been bitten by rats. Blemishes from mild but incurable acne and unhealed scars resulting from one too many shaving cuts didn't make for a pretty picture. He wasn't about to run out and buy a makeup kit; at the time it made far more sense to send her someone else's face. He found something suitable on an obscure site showcasing the photos of young and obscure literary authors. He was so giddy with the find that he didn't think to make up a name. It was only when sobriety kicked in the next morning that he realized he'd gotten it backward. She was going to see exactly what he looked like when they met, but he could've kept his real name hidden for weeks, months, or even longer. Just stupid.

And now he was stuck—stuck in a cozy wine bar. It had the capacity to seat twenty-five in the main area. It was currently seating fifteen. Avery had arrived at 3:00, thirty minutes earlier than the agreed upon meeting time, and certainly early enough to get a choice seat in the dimly lit back, facing the front door, blinking at the sunlight each time someone entered in silhouette.

Then she entered. He didn't blink. The sunlight that had shadowed all other entrants seemed to clothe her. The normally banal pink tank top and blue jeans shone like the raiment of a fairy tale princess on her. Her face glowed like a vanilla sun, just like in her picture. And her smile was straight out of a toothpaste commercial. He must've been drunk on wine fumes.

She made eye contact the moment she stepped over the threshold. Hers—implausibly—twinkled. The smile neither left her face nor changed its contours as she made her way to the table.

"Avery?"

He stood, knees wobbling as much as the three-legged table. "Charity?"

She nodded. Beauty *and* brains. Not only was she a five-foot-five bundle of hotness, she was also smart enough not to give her real name.

Avery extended his hand. She waved it away and moved in for a hug.

Disengaging from the tangle, she said, "Never worry, it *is* my real name." She winked, then took her seat and picked up the menu. "So what should we wet our tongues with first?"

Avery remained standing, unsteady. This girl, this beautiful girl, had eased into his presence as comfortably as if she'd been dating him for a year.

"Uh, there's an Oregon Pinot that's good," he said, finding his seat, not once taking his eyes off her. "It's from the Willamette Valley. Best Pinot in the New World."

"Well, far be it from me to resist the best of anything, from any world."

She peered at him over the menu. Avery was half expecting her to wink again—wink one of those twinkling eyes—but instead hers simply met his, unblinking, warming him. He flinched and looked away, resting his eyes on the table as she laid the menu down.

"You looking to call for backup?" she asked.

Avery met her eyes again, only to see hers focused on the screen of his cell. While waiting for her arrival, he'd pulled up the Freakfinder site, intending to locate and re-read her profile before meeting her. But his phone displayed the site's homepage, with its dozen squares of x-rated photos posted by shameless women.

Avery snatched the phone and jammed it into his jeans pocket. "I just wanted to remember what you looked like, so I could recognize you when you walked in."

"Well, I don't look like a vagina. And that's all I saw on your screen."

She grinned as she said it. Avery tried to chuckle in response, but it sounded more as if he were coming down with a cold than sharing a laugh.

"Besides," she said, "all I have on my profile are head shots. The number of times we've communicated, I would hope you'd have me memorized by now. You, on the other hand, were a mystery—until the last minute."

"Yeah," Avery shrugged and signaled for the waiter, "about my face pic—"

"I knew it was a fake the second I got it. Figured the body photos were, too—our little hug just now told me that they weren't. Honestly, before I came through the door, I was fully expecting to meet a woman. I just knew the name wasn't fake."

She'd said it all with a smile, not a smirk. Nevertheless, Avery couldn't help but feel embarrassed. His eyes began to drift toward the tabletop again . . . He had to shake it off. This was a once-in-a-lifetime opportunity. He had to choke back his nervousness and exude confidence. Not fake it —*believe* it.

His eyes met hers as he straightened his back. "Avery is a fake name. My real one is Chastity."

Her expression twitched as the aura around her face seemed to flicker. Avery sensed she didn't immediately get the joke. He was relieved enough when she laughed seconds later, though he was still questioning his eyesight.

They ordered their wine, and then Charity said, "Well, whoever said anyone on the net has to be who they say they are? The unwritten law is to be something completely different from reality."

"Funny thing that your name really is Charity . . . Right?"

She gave him a slow nod.

"Because, you agreeing to meet me," he said, "meet me openly and *honestly*, seems to be an act of kindness. We're from such different worlds."

"In a manner of speaking, yes. But we're not totally different. Trying to live up to the name my makers gave me, I use my spare time trying to help the unfortunate. Not too different from the volunteer work you said you do with children . . . but, then, most men on those sites claim they're athletic, kind, and attentive, with a generous sense of humor and an inclination to help others."

"Guilty of the same," Avery said, giving her his first broad smile. "And I have the evidence to prove it."

They drank, traded anecdotes, alternated bathroom breaks, and shared laughs for two hours. Avery then paid the check and escorted Charity outside.

"Can I see you again?" he asked.

"If you remember to call me, you can."

They hugged less awkwardly than before and went their separate ways. Avery walked five blocks, sobering slightly, before reaching his Honda. It had a yellow slip of paper under the wiper. He'd only put enough money in the meter for one hour, the limit. If he'd known he and Charity would hit it off so well, he would've parked in a garage.

He put the ticket in his pocket and sped home, not even caring if he was pulled over and slapped with a DUI. This had been one of the best afternoons of his life, and there was little he could think of that would ruin it.

He parked on the street, a block away from his apartment building's lot. He wanted to walk a bit more to clear his head, still in a haze from wine and thoughts of a long-term future with Charity.

He reached into his pocket for the receipt, wanting to look at the number she had scribbled on the back of it, just to make sure it was real. The receipt was there; the parking ticket was there; his smartphone was gone. He must've left it back at the bar. As fortune would have it, he'd gotten rid of his landline a year ago, so he had no way to call and ask. He decided to feed the cats, have a big glass of water, then head on back.

He pushed the button on his key to shut off the apartment's alarm. Opening the door, he almost fell backward when a pungent odor plugged his nostrils.

Avery coughed. "Sara? Cara?"

The cats didn't come when he called. Incurably shy, they always hid from strangers, running under the couch or bed whenever they heard a voice other than his. But they always came mewing when he was alone. He checked the kitchen, then under the couch. It was a one bedroom apartment, so they couldn't have gone far. He hurried into the bedroom to check under the bed. He didn't need to.

The carcasses were lying on the bed, headless and split open down the middle, their entrails removed and scattered across the bedspread. Taken together, it seemed to form some sort of pattern. Avery didn't know what, but he immediately guessed it was satanic.

He didn't have to guess much when he looked at his laptop. The cats' heads were on either side, dead-staring back at him. Whoever did this had turned the laptop on and logged into his account on Freakfinder. He stared at his profile page. It had been updated to include pictures of his face, details about his home life, and even more details about his work life. The last sentence of the About You section read: "And I kill kittens."

No telling how many subscribers to the site had seen it, but one was more than enough. Avery ignored the blood smeared on his keyboard as he hurried to delete everything. He then bolted out of his apartment for his car. While running, he tried to figure which was closer, the police station or the wine bar. Should he get his phone first, or get the cops?

Someone was leaning against his Civic. *Charity.* She wore the same smile that had dazzled him earlier, but it didn't invoke the same feelings as before. Coming from the shock in his apartment to the shock of seeing her appear from nowhere made him more nauseous than anything.

"What are you doing—?" he began.

She held up his smartphone. "You forgot this."

He didn't know where to begin. She seemed to pick up the hint.

"After we said our temporary goodbyes, I went back to the bar to ask for the name of one of the wines we had. They told me they found your phone under our table." She handed it to him. "It must've slid out of your pocket at some point."

"How did you know where I lived?"

She cocked her head. "I have your phone. You never turned it off. It was pretty easy to find your provider account info. Nothing you have on there is password protected. Not smart."

Avery switched the cell to the phone function and began dialing. "I have to call the police."

"Hey"—Charity held up her hands—"I didn't look at that much. It's not like I hacked into your bank account."

"No, someone broke into my place, and— Hello? 911? I— *Dammit*, they put me on hold!"

"Don't you have a house alarm? Why don't you just set it off? It'll probably get the cops here faster."

"Yeah, good idea." Avery hung up and turned to run back home. "I'll see you later."

It was much later when he realized there were probably better ideas, like staying on the line. But thinking straight had been a problem for him all day. Only that night, after the cops left, did he wonder how much digging Charity had actually done on his cell phone, and why she seemed so positive his apartment had an alarm—an alarm whose deactivation code was stored in his phone's list of computer and email passwords.

MONDAY at the office began the way of all Monday mornings, with a surly mood permeating the air, one that would only begin to dissipate once everyone had gotten halfway through their first cup of coffee. Avery and most of his fellow middle managers were already on their second cups. He anticipated he'd be on his fourth by the time someone from the police department called to let him know how the investigation was going. It was a new—and ironic—department policy: all victims were required to be notified of their case's status within twenty-four hours, whether or not there'd been any progress. After that, it was the victim's responsibility to follow up. Avery considered it ironic due to the open secret of how leisurely the department operated.

He'd gotten little sleep. It wasn't just that he slept on the stiff leather couch (there was no way in hell he was going anywhere near the bed), but he couldn't stop thinking about potential culprits. Who were his enemies? Who hated him so much that they'd break into his house and not steal or break anything but kill his closest companions and try to ruin his reputation? What the hell had he ever done to anyone?

He moved the cursor to open an email that popped into his inbox, then his screen went black. Seconds later it came to back to life, showing his Freakfinder profile page bright as day. Avery panicked as he heard others around him gasping. He quickly looked over both shoulders. No one was peering through the entranceway to his cubicle; none of his neighbors were peering through the walls, staring at his screen.

Middle manager status notwithstanding, he and everyone else who did work of middling relevance sat within the labyrinth of cubicles that covered most of the football-field-sized floor. Only the top dogs got the offices lining the walls, while the lower levels got a seat on the long tables in the center of the room. But no one remained hidden. Glass and mostly transparent plastic composed the office and cubicle walls. Part of the trends of the decade: shorter buildings, bigger floors, and transparency. And nosier coworkers.

Avery thought—hoped, *prayed*—he'd imagined the gasps and subsequent chatter. Or, if real, that it was due to something he wasn't seeing. What he was seeing now was having the jittering effect of ten coffees, particularly since the profile was the doctored page he thought he'd deleted.

Then as now, he banged away at his keyboard, trying to get the image off his screen before anyone saw. Nothing worked. He could scroll up and down, taking in all the pictures, all the lurid prose describing his dreams and desires and proclivities, but he couldn't click away from the page. He couldn't even reduce its size. As he prepared to jam his finger into the power button, the screen went blank. Seconds later, he was staring at his work email again.

No gasps from him or anyone else this time, just his own heavy sigh of relief. He prepared to open the email that had popped into his inbox a few minutes ago when he noticed a new one. Subject line: Ready to meet your new Match? Sender: Adult Freakfinder.

Shit. He received such messages through a personal email account he'd set up for this very purpose. When trying to delete his account on Sunday, had he mistakenly typed in his work email address?

He deleted the message unread and picked up his desk phone. He needed a distraction. He needed to take his eyes off his computer for a few minutes. He called the police department's non-emergency number and was put on hold, then bounced around for five minutes, until he was finally transferred to someone who could give him an update.

"We were going to call you this afternoon."

"I know," Avery said, "but I just couldn't wait."

"Well, we have news, but it's nothing that's going to reassure you."

Avery sighed. "Of course. Nothing about the last twenty-four hours has been reassuring."

"There was no forced entry into your place. No fingerprints anywhere, other than yours. And out of the people we've been able to talk to so far, none of them saw anything or anyone suspicious around your building."

The officer didn't say it, but Avery got the implication. So far, he was the only suspect in the slaughter of his cats and the attempt to ruin his reputation.

"If you want any additional updates," the officer said. "Please come down to the station and ask in person."

Of course.

Avery hung up as an announcement came over the intercom, booming through the warehouse-sized room. "Mr. Avery Brocus, a Mr. Charity Mansion is here to see you. Please come to the reception area."

Avery shook his head. *Charity*? Was "Mansion" her last name? And what was up with the "mister"? He couldn't have heard all of that right. His ears had to be deceiving him; but his eyes . . .

His cubicle—maybe luckily, maybe not—wasn't that far from the reception area. His knees wobbled like gelatin as he slowly stood, peering over the cubicle wall. Many others around him were doing the same. Something in the pit of his stomach told him what to expect. But after his eyes scanned and met those of the visitor, the dreadful feeling in his stomach dropped lower, inciting nausea.

The tall man seemed to be in his mid- to late fifties—it was hard to tell as he clearly spent a lot of time in the sun, undoubtedly on a Harley. His orangish skin and biker jacket weren't the only giveaways. The shades, bandana, and white horseshoe mustache completed the look. The man was beefy, and he stood in a manner suggesting he was concealing something in his jacket, something long and made of metal.

This was some sick joke. His coworkers certainly thought so, doing little to conceal their snickers and chortles as Avery shuffled through the labyrinth toward the reception area. He considered running off in a different direction, but he couldn't think of a safe destination.

"Hello, Mr. Brocus." The biker's voice was as raspy as Avery had assumed.

Avery stammered and coughed once before asking, "Can I help you?"

"You've already started," the biker said with a sneer. "You

agreed to make a donation to Charity, Brocus. And I will have Mercy on your soul when it is complete."

Avery shook his head. "I'm afraid I don't—"

"Excuse me for attempting to be polite for the sake of the ladies"—he nodded toward the four middle-aged receptionists occupying one long desk—"but I was talking about my wife, you little fucker."

Avery swallowed and tried to steady his knees and his voice. "Sir, this is a place of business."

"Yes," he said with a growl, "and I'm here to discuss you sticking yours into mine."

All four receptionists regarded the two men with expressions of stark horror. Avery felt like they looked but tried to keep a brave face as he said, "Maybe we'd better talk at my desk."

"Yeah." The biker nodded and turned toward the cubicle maze as Avery read the stitchwork on the back of his jacket: Hell's Mercy. He sure hoped for mercy as he led the potential neckbreaker toward his desk.

This was Charity's husband? The pairing made no sense. Even if true, was this guy so jealous that he'd threaten or beat Avery just for having wine with the woman? *That* made a little more sense. If he looked like this guy and was able to pull a woman like Charity, he would jealously guard her too.

But Avery *had* a woman like Charity. At least, he was on the verge of getting her. Why couldn't *he* be the one to jealously guard her? She was special enough to fight for. In the brief amount of time he'd spent with her, she'd made him feel like a new man, reinvigorated; his desire for older women had been wiped away by one much younger woman. His thing for older women may've been sourced from a deep down desire to be taught in some secret, beautiful, pleasure that only an older, wiser woman could give him. That was a childish fantasy. A *perverse* fantasy. But his interest in Charity seemed more natural, more correct, something he wouldn't have to hide. Modern society would tolerate an older man with a younger woman. Nod at, smile at, and applaud it.

But to keep a woman like her—a once-in-a-lifetime opportunity—he'd have to shake this bruiser off. He'd again have choke back his nervousness and exude confidence. Not fake it—*believe* it. And then do something with it.

He steered the biker around twists and turns easily navigable only by long-term employees. Avery was no longer headed toward his little space but toward the grander area in the middle, where all the lower level employees sat at the long tables working on their tablets and laptops. If anything happened, security personnel could respond to this area quicker. There were four routes that cut directly through the maze.

Avery stopped and tried staring through the man's shades. "Whatever we have to discuss, we might as well discuss it here."

The biker looked around, meeting the glances of the curious employees who quickly pretended they found their work more interesting than him.

"Okay, pal. Looks like I've got you right where I want you."

"Listen. Charity and I only—"

"Charity and *I*, we make something of a wonderful team, see." He removed his shades. "We specialize in giving people, not what they want, but what they really need."

The man had no irises, no pupils. Black marbles with golden swirls filled his eyesockets.

Avery stepped backward. "What the fuck are you?"

"A philosopher." He smiled the same smile Charity had

a day before. "One who has studied and examined your kind. Inside and out. Look around you. Look at where you've chosen to spend the majority of your waking hours. An illusion of order—similar clothing, identical workspaces, the caste levels . . . And at the same time, an illusion of disorder —a maze filled with messy work stations, hungover office drones overqualified for their meaningless activities . . ."

A philosopher, maybe. Typical biker, certainly not. Avery couldn't help but look the man in the eyes as he responded; he was less scared than in awe. "I just work here. I had nothing to do with setting anything, *any* of this up. And what does this have to do with Charity?"

The biker smirked. "Swimming in illusions, and dying of thirst. Your kind is *wanting*, man. You offered yourself to Charity, so I'm offering you Mercy."

He raised both arms above his head and snapped his fingers. The lights and computers blinked. An orange haze tinged the air while, on each nearby laptop screen, Avery saw photoshopped pictures of him in a variety of compromising situations and positions with old women and young boys. Each screen held a lurid picture for a few seconds before flashing to another regrettable one.

The office was in an uproar. The images were apparently on every screen. Many people screamed about lost work; the rest screamed about the disgusting images flashing before their eyes.

"Wh— Stop! Why are you doing this? *How* are you doing this? *Stop* it!" Avery's pleas and questions were met with a grin as the biker's sunbaked face paled and emitted a faint glow that steadily grew brighter.

"Your nervous system," the biker said, "the human nervous system imposed all these illusions of Order and Disorder on the universe—but illusions aren't true. An objective perspective of the truth can only be obtained by giving to Charity and accepting Mercy."

It was only then that Avery realized the biker was referring to himself as Mercy. And it was then, amid the pandemonium, that he saw all of his coworkers looking at him, switching their gazes between him and their computer screens, screaming out of disgust, screaming about lost documents, hollering insults. Even the big shots were coming out of their offices and making their own vocal contributions to the madness.

Avery turned for the nearest exit, but the biker's arm shot forward like a frog's tongue; his hand around Avery's throat was just as sticky. Avery was forced to look into those gold-streaked eyes as the biker challenged him.

"This is the *crux* of giving and receiving. Those who've been abused by the images, the ordered and disordered details of your life, they're limited to the people in this wide, wide room. I've blocked the exits. Only these people know your secrets, true and false. So you, in your heightened state of anxiety, have a choice. Shall I kill them and let only you go? Or shall I let all of you live with what you've all seen?"

The biker was correct—Avery was now more nervous, more *scared* than he'd ever been. The choice at first seemed a ridiculous one, until he repeated it to himself for the fifth time. In neither case would this, this *Mercy*, kill his body. It was a choice between the death of his conscience and morals, by ordering all his coworkers dead, or the death of his reputation and ultimately—*probably*—his sanity, wondering at all times what all these people, former friends and acquaintances, might be thinking about him.

"You have five seconds."

Five seconds before what? Which choice would this

tiger-eyed psychotic take? Avery couldn't risk staying silent. He'd make his own choice.

"Kill m—"

The biker choked the remainder away. "Time's up," he smirked. "And I heard: kill *many*." He released his hold.

Before Avery could regain his breath, let alone speak a word of protest, the biker darted at three or four times the speed of a tiger into the labyrinth of cubicles, snatching each man or woman within reach and, with blinding speed, thrusting his hands into their backs, lighting up their bodies and ripping out their spines before moving on to the next one.

Avery was too frightened to run anywhere. The biker, the *whatever*, was moving faster and faster as he went— running and ripping, lighting up bodies as if they were lamps before unplugging them. There was no escape for Avery or anyone else. He would just have to wait where he was, waiting to meet his fate after all the others.

He had a hard time making sense of any of the past twenty-four hours' happenings. As everyone else ran around screaming, he numbly watched Mercy darting through the labyrinth like a grotesque version of the fabled and already grotesque Minotaur. He just as numbly turned his eyes upward to see the ripple in the air near the ceiling, several dozen feet up, and the violet man-sized eagle materializing through it like stained light through a closed window.

The sight of an eagle comprised of violet flames was only in his view for a few seconds before it entered the labyrinth like a bundle of hopping sparks, evading every living person until meeting Mercy head on. The violet bird then flared, shooting itself out of the maze and into the air above Avery, close to the area where it had initially appeared. Two flaming talons held Mercy by his arms, but the one-time biker had no time to either struggle or say a word before the bird flipped him and flung him down. Mercy crashed through a table adjacent to Avery's, hollering as any mortal would after being thrown with enough force to break wood two inches thick.

Mercy was immobilized, done for. But that didn't stop the violet bird of light from swooping down to snatch him by the throat and lift him out of the debris.

Avery watched the giant bird shift its form, resolving itself into something with human-like arms and legs. The spanning wings of violet light remained as the beak shifted to a helmet's position on a head appearing more wolf-like than anything. The eight-foot being pulled the marble-eyed biker within a few inches of its canine snout.

"I have mercy on your soul." The creature of light spoke with a voice enveloped in thunder before streams of light shot from its head into the biker's eyes, ears, nostrils, and mouth. The biker's skin turned cloud-white with graying spots as it sunk in on itself. The streams of light seemed to act as proboscises, shifting through various hues of red as they sucked the life out of the biker, withering his skin until it appeared as an ash-colored raisin. Finished, the violet creature dropped the corpse back into the mess of splintered wood and broken laptops and turned toward Avery.

"Where's the other one?"

The rumbling voice didn't stifle all the screaming and terrified expressions, but it quieted the room. Or maybe Avery was so tuned in to this wondrous being addressing him that his attention hadn't much for anyone else around him. He was also speechless. The violet being was impatient.

It stepped toward Avery, shifting its appearance again, wiping away the violet flames covering its visage, shape-shifting its face into that of a man with vanilla-violet skin and deep purple eyes. Its body remained robed in ruffles of light that, in such close proximity, Avery now knew was simply *light*—though maybe not *simply*, but definitely not flames, despite the appearance. The only warmth Avery felt was from his own nervousness, nervousness preventing him from fleeing as well as speaking, a nervousness anyone would feel when addressed by an eight-foot-tall angel.

"Avery Brocus," the angel said, "where is the other one?"

"I— Other—?"

The angel closed the distance, standing no more than a few feet in front of Avery. Avery swallowed as he looked into those soul-sucking eyes.

"What is happening?"

"You opened a line of communication with demons," the angel said. "They were beginning a ritual, using you as the focal point."

"This . . . guy? A demon?"

"I have another word for his kind, but 'demon' is the apt term for your understanding. They work in pairs. They present themselves as artists or philosophers, walking works of beauty or fascination. In reality, they make fools of their subjects; they then kill the bodies and extinguish the souls of those connected to the fool, as many as possible at one time."

Avery nodded. "So I'm the fool." He should've known someone like Charity wouldn't be interested in him as a man, or even as a human being. He'd been scammed by someone out to bruise his psyche and rob him of his very core.

"Their minds and souls were shaped in another dimension," the angel said. "Their philosophies and art are incomprehensible to those in your realm. Each pair of demons has unique methods, but these two targeted men and women looking for *love*, then psychologically tormented them in a compressed amount of time in order to feed off of their psychic energy. Heightened anxiety, fear, embarrassment, and confusion, all of it released with a psychic deathscream, satiates them."

"And, you," Avery said. "You're a guardian angel? Out to protect me and the other fools?"

"I am Valentinus. I am out to correct errors and save the chosen for the Hereafter."

Avery shook his head. "It's like something out of the Book of Revelation."

"No," Valentinus said. "A new book is being written about The End. About *now*."

Avery's eyes dropped to the floor. Today was his own personal Judgment Day—and what a life . . . What a fucking life he'd led. He'd trudged through school, got a boring job, and took even less interesting vacations. And then, after— he *thought*—finally getting in touch with himself, he set out on a curving road to satisfy an admittedly odd craving; detoured, he opened a gate leading to Hell. The punishment didn't fit the crime. But, what *was* the crime?

"What now?" he asked.

"I must deal with the damaged souls here," Valentinus said. "But I must deal with the other demon afterward. Go out and find her. *Hold* her. I am sure she will hone in on you."

Valentinus leapt into the air and hovered near the ceiling. Avery was half expecting to see a patch of air rippling near the angel. Instead, the rippling patch appeared near Avery, off to his right. A portal, he surmised, that would get him out of here. He stepped toward it, then paused to look at Valentinus as the angel flared, sending out innumerable streamers of violet light. He saw the light piercing the faces of his nearby colleagues. They didn't scream, but their bodies were rapidly transfigured, twisting like pretzels in the making. Not wanting to be next, Avery ran into the portal.

THE PORTAL DEPOSITED Avery on the steps outside the police station. He was surprised it worked as he'd wished it would, but shocked the portal didn't place him right outside his workplace. When running through the tear in the air, he'd thought of running to the police. Something had read his mind and made the task easy by not forcing him to run. The difficulty was in trying to talk to the police. They rolled their eyes at the mention of demons and angels. It was only after they demanded he leave the station or be locked up that he realized he should've simply said that his coworkers were under attack; he shouldn't have jammed that statement at the end of one confirming the existence of the inhabitants of Heaven and Hell on Earth.

He trudged home, taking the time halfway to make a 911 call on his smartphone. *Workplace massacre—please hurry.* Whatever happened next, happened.

When it was within sight, he headed toward one of his building's side entrances, the one closest to his apartment. Charity was leaning against a nearby tree. Seeing her in skimpy blue jean shorts and a pink crop top, an outfit cut and created out of her previous one, Avery almost began to feel for her all over again. He truly was a fool.

"Why?" he asked when within non-shouting distance.

She straightened. Appearing genuinely confused, she looked in his eyes. "Why what?"

"Why did I have to be the one to let this loose?"

He knew he shouldn't have said it. He should've acted like nothing was wrong. He should've smiled and waved upon seeing her, suggested they walk to the nearest coffee shop, and there he'd keep her until Valentinus arrived. But in her presence, his pride overwhelmed good sense.

"What are you talking about?" Charity asked.

"You." He gazed hard into her blue-shimmering eyes as his brow furrowed. "Demons."

"Oh." She turned away, toward the shrubbery. "He came."

"Yes," Avery said. "Your so-called husband came and ripped apart my coworkers."

"What?" She again looked into his eyes; hers seemed to be on the edge of fury. "Valentinus is *not* my husband!"

Avery shook his head. "No—*Mercy*—the biker! The philoso— You *know* who I'm talking about!"

"He's Valentinus's herald," Charity said. "He appears before Valentinus. He breaks up bodies—physically and psychically—so Valentinus can suck out the souls."

Avery gaped at her. He didn't know what to say. He'd been shoved into a battle between angels and demons and wasn't sure which was which. Everything he'd witnessed over the past several hours had been unbelievable before being plausibly explained by the violet angel. But now, what Charity was saying, coupled with what he'd seen the violet one do . . . Valentinus could just have easily been the real evildoer.

"I'll be honest with you," Charity said. "I found you online and established contact because I knew Valentinus was zeroing in on you, following your electronic movements. He's a demon that feeds on those who make 'errors' in love; those who don't stick to what is true and proper. I was hoping to reach out to you in time, to protect you. When I went through your phone yesterday, I was trying to find a way to trace and locate him while he was spying on you from another dimension. I wasn't successful."

"But— Why did you kill my cats?"

"I didn't kill your cats, Avery. If anyone did, it was Mercy, setting up the beginning of a ritual feast for him and Valentinus."

"Why should I believe you?"

"Look at me." Her eyes twinkled as they had on Sunday. It wasn't a trick on his eyes. She wasn't fully human. "Avery, *I* am the angel. *They* are the demons. Weigh our appearances. Think about the fate of your coworkers."

They were probably all dead, snuffed away to oblivion. Avery was the sole survivor, living his life, the life he always lived—going along only to be tricked in one direction then kicked in another. A fool.

"I came here to see how you were, waiting till you got off work. I should've come by this morning. But you're alive, and Valentinus will be coming to finish what he started. Here." She reached into her shorts pocket and pulled out a ring with a large mounted diamond. It had to be worth a small fortune. She handed it to him. "Put this on your finger. I'm limited in what I can do against him. I may not be able to beat him. At most, I will probably distract him. If I do, *punch* him. Thrust the diamond into his eye. It will extinguish him."

Avery looked at the ring, wondering. He was about to ask her why she didn't wear it when nerves scratched at the back of his neck. He instinctively looked up to see the air shimmering just above the top of the tree. Valentinus appeared like before, a giant eagle composed of violet fire, but he readily shifted into an angelic posture as he descended, landing on the grass a couple dozen feet away from them.

"Your time is up, Errorist," he thundered. "Your partner has been subdued. Much of your power is gone."

Charity looked at Valentinus warily, then at Avery. Her eyes twinkled as she grabbed him by the shoulders, pulled, and gave him a passionate kiss. She pulled away and whispered, "I'm sorry you were caught up in this."

Valentinus approached. "Never again."

Charity looked at him, more resolved, and stepped forward. "You're forgetting—"

"I have forgotten nothing," he thundered.

"You're forgetting," Charity repeated, "*you* made me."

"In another lifetime," Valentinus said. "I made a mistake. I'm correcting it now."

Charity pointed at him, her arms like rifles. Or maybe more like leaf blowers. Somehow she blew away much of the violet light enveloping Valentinus, making him appear as a mere giant of a man, naked, with a violet-tinged vanilla hue.

She glanced at Avery. "Remember—"

Valentinus darted in and grabbed her by the forearms. Charity hardly had time to look him in the face before he snapped her arms like matchsticks. The woman loosed an unearthly scream that Avery was sure would be heard blocks away, maybe even all the way to the police station.

But no one was coming to the rescue. Time was crucial. Mercy had given him a choice between two options; he'd tried to choose a third, and it didn't turn out so well. Charity didn't really give him an explicit choice, but . . . Each man and woman would have a personal Judgment Day— compressed chaos, and a *split second* to make a final decision.

Avery ran at the two and lunged. Before either could flinch, he punched the jewel into the eye.

Charity fell backward onto the grass, grinning without sound, until her mouth froze into a wide smile displaying off-white teeth.

"Why did you do that?"

Avery looked up, into the otherworldly purple irises of Valentinus.

"I did as she asked," Avery said. "*Remembered.* All that she'd said. She was full of contradictions. Inconsistencies. She was a classic scammer. All the time I was with her I was nervous, anxious, and she was feeding off of it. I didn't fully trust her."

"And yet you did exactly what she wanted you to do."

Avery shook his head. "She wanted me to do this—*that* —to you."

Valentinus looked at the ring on Avery's finger. "That wouldn't have hurt me." He held up his left hand; a diamond and gold ouroboros twisted around the angel's middle and ring fingers. "She knew it would have no effect on me or else she would've done it herself. What you've done is extinguish her soul, preventing me from taking it."

Avery stared at the diamond ring on his own finger. *Fool.* Scammed again. How many more times?

"Her soul has dissipated in a fashion that makes it impossible to recollect." Valentinus looked at Avery as he reassumed his robes of ruffling light. "I needed to pair her soul with her partner's."

"Why?" Avery stepped forward, curiosity overwhelming his fear. "*Why?*"

"Books are being written. Plots are being tilled. A harmonious Hereafter is not a foregone conclusion." He turned his piercing eyes to Avery.

Avery recoiled at a realization. "No . . . No *way*!"

"You accepted her ring, and her kiss. You must reap what you sow."

"But— But I never really had a choice! Not a fair one!"

"You make a choice each time you take a breath, even if you believe it's involuntary."

"Fine," Avery shouted, "then I'm telling you with all the breath I have left that I refuse to let you take me!"

"You are out of choices."

Avery lowered his head, shaking it. "Not fair . . ."

"That's always been the way of life. Its end rushes at you. A minor sin overwhelms you, buries you, sends you to where you don't think you deserve to go, because you've really done nothing . . . But now, there's me. I offer redemption. Your life won't be quick, dirty, and meaningless. I am giving you a chance to take part in a minor plot to save a world."

Avery raised his head. He hadn't completely lost the will to protest, but he was losing it, along with the slivers of skin he felt being peeled from him like an onion as he wept, gazing into those eyes, striped violet and gold, unspooling . . . . The angel's gaze made Avery more cognizant of something within himself, something deep within, something the remaining fragments of his here-and-now consciousness could only describe as a glob of honey. His *soul*. Avery was being stripped down to his bare essence, a realization that struck him before the angel's eyes flashed and he felt memories—every memory of every second of his life—flash-flooding through him before his very heart was snatched out and his consciousness blacked out.

∾

THE ROUTINE BEGAN like it always began—without beginning. There was no day or night in the vineyard maze, only chores to perform, another dimension's soil to cultivate. As near as Avery could tell, thousands of souls were working on this one plot. His soul and that of the one once known as Mercy worked together. All souls were required to pair up. And Mercy, reformed as he had been, was an ideal partner.

Here, Avery's once deep-down desire had been mostly fulfilled. As they worked, he and the other souls were taught pleasing, beautiful secrets that only something much wiser than any human of any known gender or age could give him. It was no childish fantasy; it was a ripening and wonderful reality. A new world was coming.

Presently, he paused his work to gaze upward. The immobile thousand-foot-tall giant at whose feet he worked had the body of a human woman. Never mind there were no actual humans in this realm—there were only angels, their enemies, and once-human souls. Inside the giant's head were angels, guiding, making schemes and preparations to ensure they and their chosen ones survived the erasure of Earth and its universe. The angels were trusted completely. No soul under them would even consider doubting their devices.

In the labyrinthine vineyard of unearthly delights, Avery was happy to be a slave, a stripped-naked soul. There was so much that would not be understood until after the final Revelation unfolded, ushering in the Hereafter, but he was secure in the knowledge he'd never again be anyone's—or anything's—*fool*.

ABOUT THE SERIES

Eve of Light is a Dark Metaphysical Fantasy series chronicling the surreal events leading up to the Apocalypse—the Death of God. The setting is a contemporary, alternate Earth on the verge of a cataclysm that will warp space, time, and minds. The main narrative of those plotting and battling to save humanity is told in the *Eve of Light* series of novels. The short stories and novellas are simply flashes on the fringe—episodes told from the perspective of everyday men and women living in a world turned weird.

The Core Novels

Stories on the Fringe

ABOUT THE AUTHOR

Harambee K. Grey-Sun writes under the broad umbrella of speculative fiction. He integrates elements of fantasy, horror, noir, black humor, and science fiction into his work and spins dark, surreal, mysterious, grotesque, at times challenging, and often blasphemous tales. Many of his stories can be categorized into one or more of the following subgenres: speculative thriller, urban fantasy, metaphysical fantasy, superhero, occult/supernatural, slipstream, and–*of course*– weird fiction. His Dark Metaphysical Fantasy series *Eve of Light* examines the dark nature of God and what it really means to be human.

For more information:
www.harambeegreysun.com